Spot Goes Splash!
and other stories

Eric Hill

Grosset & Dunlap, Publishers

First published in *Spot's Bedtime Storybook* by G.P. Putnam's Sons, 1998.

Copyright © 1998 by Eric Hill. All rights reserved. Published in 2000 by Grosset & Dunlap, a division of Penguin Putnam Books for Young Readers, New York. GROSSET & DUNLAP is a trademark of Grosset & Dunlap, Inc. Planned and produced by Ventura Publishing Ltd., 27 Wrights Lane, London W8 5TZ, England. Published simultaneously in Canada. Printed in the U.S.A.

Library of Congress Cataloging-in-Publication Data is available.

ISBN 0-448-42091-0   A B C D E F G H I J

Spot
Goes
Splash!

It was raining when Spot woke up.
"Oh, dear," he thought. "I'll have to stay indoors.
I wonder what Steve and Helen are doing today?"
"Breakfast is ready," Sally called from the kitchen.
Spot loved breakfast. He forgot all about the rain.

After he had finished eating, Spot looked outside again.
"Oh, good," he said. "It's stopped raining. Can I go outside and play, Mom?"
"All right," Sally told him. "But don't get all wet and muddy. I've just cleaned the house because Grandma and Grandpa are coming to visit."

Spot went out into the garden. The sun was beginning
to shine. Spot saw Steve looking up at the sky.
"Do you see the rainbow, Spot?" asked Steve.
"Yes!" said Spot. "It's so many different colors."

Helen came along wearing a raincoat,
a big rain hat, and shiny red rubber boots.
"It's stopped raining, Helen," said Spot.
"I know," said Helen.

"You don't need your raincoat and hat and boots anymore," Steve told her.

"Yes, I do," said Helen, smiling. "Especially the boots. I need them to walk through puddles. Like this…" And she stomped through a big puddle. *Splash!*

"That looks like fun!" said Spot.
"Let's try it!" said Steve. And they splashed
through the puddles, too, stomping and shouting.
"You two are silly," said Helen. "Now your feet
are all wet and muddy."
"We don't care," they said. "This is great!"

"It's starting to rain again," said Helen. "I'm still nice and dry, and you two will have to go home."
"I suppose so," said Spot, having one last splash.

By the time he got home, Spot was
very wet and very muddy.
Sally was not pleased.
"Get into the bath at once," she said.
"But it's not time to go to bed yet,"
said Spot.
"I know," said Sally, "but it's time
for a bath."

So Spot got into the tub with his boat and
toy duck.
"This is fun, too," he thought. "Now when
Grandma and Grandpa come, the house
will be all clean, and so will I!"

Spot
at the
Fair

Grandma and Grandpa
took Spot to the fair.
"What would you like
to go on first, Spot?"
"I'd like to go on the
merry-go-round,"
said Spot.
Grandpa lifted Spot
up onto the horse.
"You too, Grandma and
Grandpa," said Spot.

"This is fun," Grandpa
said.
Grandma agreed.
"Ooh, I can't remember
when I last did this."

"What next, Spot?" asked Grandma. Spot looked around. "I'd like to go on the slide," he said.

Spot came whizzing down. "Wheee!"
"I'd like to go on that," said Grandpa.
"Me too," said Grandma.

Grandma came down the slide followed
by Grandpa.
"This is great, Spot. What a time
we're having!"
Spot laughed to see his grandparents
having so much fun. Then he went
on the slide again.

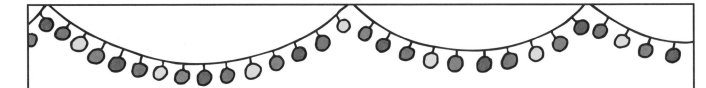

"Can I go on the bumper cars now?" Spot asked.
"I'll sit with you," said Grandma.
"I'll just watch," said Grandpa.

A loud buzz sounded and Spot pushed
down on the pedal. They were off.
"There's Helen and Tom!" shouted Spot.
"Hold on tight, Grandma," said Spot, as
Helen bumped her car into theirs.
Bang!

"My word," said Grandma,
"this is some ride!"
Then Spot bumped Helen's car.
"That's the fun of it," said Spot,
laughing. *Bang!*

When the ride finished, Spot and Grandma
climbed out of the car.
"That was a little scary," said Grandma.
"It was," said Spot, "but sometimes it's
fun to be a little scared."

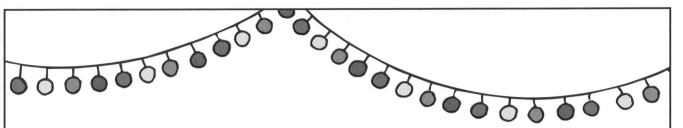

"Where's Grandpa?" asked Grandma. He was nowhere in sight.
Suddenly Helen pointed. "I think I can see him. He's carrying something big and pink."

"Where have you been?" said Grandma.
"We were worried."
"I got bored waiting so I tried my luck
on the ball toss. I won this for Spot."
"Wow!" said Spot, as he licked the cotton
candy Grandpa had bought. "Way to go,
Grandpa! Thanks for a lovely fun day."
"Thank *you*, Spot," said Grandpa. "We
enjoyed it as much as you did."

Sweet Dreams, Spot

It was the start of a busy day.
After breakfast, Spot went with his mom
to do the shopping. There was a long list
of things to get.
"Thank you, Spot," said Sally. "I couldn't
have done all this without your help."

After lunch, he went to
the park with his dad.
At the playground, Spot
went on the swings.
"Push me higher, Dad!"
said Spot.

When Spot and his dad got home from the park, Helen, Tom, and Steve came over to play hide-and-seek.

Finally, as it was getting dark, Spot's friends went home to bed. Spot was ready for bed, too.

After Spot had had his supper, he
went for a last walk in the garden.
A small voice said, "Hello, Spot,
have you come out to play?"
"No, I'm going to bed," said Spot.
"Oh well," said the mole,
"sleep tight."

As Spot walked by the pond, he heard a frog croak.
"Hello, Spot. It's a lovely evening for a swim."
"Not for me, thanks. I'm off to bed," said Spot.

"Tu-whit, tu-whoo!" hooted the owl.
"Good night, Owl," said Spot.
"What do you mean good night?"
the owl asked. "I've just woken
up. I've got lots to do."
"Not me," Spot yawned.
"I've had a busy day."

Spot went back indoors.
Spot kissed his dad. "I've had
a lovely day, Dad. Thanks for
taking me to the park."
"Good night, Spot," said Sam.

Sally came in to kiss Spot good night.
"Read me a story, Mom," said Spot.
Sally opened the book and started to read.

Spot snuggled down, cozy
and warm. He got sleepier
and sleepier. By the time
the story was over, Spot
was fast asleep.

"What a tired little puppy!" Sally whispered. "I didn't realize that I've been reading the story and there was no one listening."

"Oh yes, there was," said a voice. Sally looked around and there on the windowsill were the owl, the frog, and the mole.

"Thanks for the story, Sally," they said. "And sweet dreams, Spot."

Spot opened one eye. "Yes, thanks, Mom," he said. "Good night, everyone." And he fell fast asleep again.